大鵬鳥學飛記

文／孟瑛如
圖／閻寧
英文翻譯／吳侑達

大鵬鳥是群鳥之王，身體常同時有紅綠雙色羽毛，體型巨大！

大鵬鳥是《西遊記》中獅駝國的三大王，被稱為「雲程萬里鵬」，能夠力搏大風，翻攪海浪！

在《辛巴達歷險記》中，主角辛巴達第二次出海時被棄置在孤島，情急之下將自己繫在大鵬鳥的鳥爪上，靠著大鵬鳥逃到高崖之巔。他在那裡看見了巨大的鳥蛋，也發現大鵬鳥以巨蟒為食。

辛巴達第五次航行時又在一座島上發現大鵬鳥蛋，同行的商人打破蛋殼爭食。大鵬鳥爸爸媽媽回來時看到這情景心痛不已，勃然大怒下用強壯的腳爪搬運巨石將商船擊沉。

大鵬鳥還是中國著名詩人李白傳誦千古名句中的主角——「大鵬一日同風起，扶搖直上九萬里」。而我們也常聽到所謂「鵬程萬里」這句話，所以大鵬鳥一向是志向高遠、豪放氣概的象徵。

隨著時間的演變，大鵬鳥的棲息地越來越不足，族群也因此越來越少。同時由於牠的翅膀太大太長，起飛時，下方必須有大風相助，大鵬鳥才能借助風力向上飛行，就像是大船要借助深水才能浮起一樣，所以必須要住在高聳且空曠的山崖上，才能隨時有大風協助飛行！

當大鵬鳥爸媽越來越找不到築巢的地方，生的蛋就越來越少；生的蛋越少，能存活下來的大鵬鳥寶寶也就更顯珍貴。每隻大鵬鳥爸媽都越來越寵愛自己的寶寶，捨不得他們吃一點苦，所以大部分的大鵬鳥寶寶不會築窩，有時睡覺還會摔出鳥巢受傷；他們也不會抓蛇吃，甚至許多蛇都敢在大鵬鳥寶寶面前囂張的爬來爬去，因為知道消失野性的大鵬鳥寶寶是拿自己沒辦法的。

不過，有件事對大鵬鳥來說，可是一件「鳥」生大事，那就是學習飛行！

大鵬鳥鵬鵬的爸媽出自大鵬鳥族群裡極有聲望的家族，他們只有鵬鵬這個孩子，因此他自小備受寵愛。鵬鵬對如何御風飛行這件事始終找不到訣竅，爸媽又很怕他受傷，在教鵬鵬學飛時總是綁手綁腳的，不敢真的放手讓他飛，但越不敢放手，鵬鵬對飛行就越沒有信心！

鵬鵬花在學飛的時間比其他大鵬鳥寶寶都長，這讓鵬鵬的爸媽在族群裡沒面子極了！連山崖上的小鳥們都嘲笑鵬鵬：「我們這些小鳥兒，要起飛就起飛，要降落就降落，不必像你們這種大鵬鳥還要等待起風時，才能順風而飛。再說，我們這種小鳥兒，高興時就飛到樹上，有時也可以飛到地面，哪像你們還得飛到九萬里的高空上？」

鵬鵬被小鳥奚落一番之後更加不敢飛了，反而用巨大的翅膀去搧搧樹，用強壯的腳爪在岩石上走來走去，表示自己也是行動自如、能夠獨立生活的大鳥。這讓鵬鵬的爸媽更加著急，鵬鵬的爸爸嚴肅的對鵬鵬說：「我們是鳥中之王，小鳥兒飛得不高，因此看得也比較近，就像一種早上才出生，但到了夜晚便死亡的小蟲，牠無法看到一年四季的不同變化。我們一向飛得高，所以看到的世界也會不同；別人不一定了解我們，我們自己才了解自己。明天再加強訓練吧！」

在小鳥嘲笑事件之後，鵬鵬的爸媽擔心他再被嘲笑，所以都等眾鳥回巢後才開始在夜間訓練鵬鵬。每晚，月光下的山崖邊，總有兩隻急切暴躁的大鳥和一隻呵欠連連的鳥寶寶忙著練習飛行的身影。

鵬鵬的爸媽因為擔心他受傷，所以不敢像從前自己的爸媽訓練他們時，先講解好訣竅及規則，然後就直接用強壯的腳爪將孩子慢慢推下山崖，讓孩子自己感受風向與風速如何鼓動翅膀，以及御風飛行的感覺；就算重摔落地或是被山崖邊的樹枝纏住，也只是拍拍塵土，嬉鬧一陣再重來。鵬鵬爸媽這一代都是這樣經歷無數次挫折與失敗而學會飛行的，爺爺奶奶在訓練鵬鵬爸媽飛行時最常說的話是：「哪有練習飛行不摔個幾次的？摔倒沒關係，能夠再爬起來就好！畢竟我們是大鵬鳥啊！」

鵬鵬的爸媽怕鵬鵬摔落地面，所以用一條繩子拴著他脖子，爸爸在前面銜著繩子助跑後飛行，媽媽在後面幫忙用力推鵬鵬。鵬鵬如果跑得不夠快，爸爸已銜著繩子飛起時，他就會被拴在脖子上的繩子勒到上氣不接下氣；在後面的媽媽如果心急推得太猛烈，鵬鵬又會跌個狗吃屎！就這樣，兩大一小三隻鳥常在月光下相互抱怨或是累到說不出話來。

鵬鵬的爸媽覺得再這樣下去不是辦法，決定試一試自己小時候被訓練的方法。一個月黑風高的晚上，再三叮嚀鵬鵬後，爸爸小心翼翼的用腳爪將鵬鵬輕輕推下山崖，鵬鵬腳一離地，覺得自己沒有跟對風勢，不自覺的「啊！」慘叫一聲。鵬鵬的爸媽心一緊，忘了要讓孩子自己摸索御風訣竅的初衷，立刻一左一右飛到鵬鵬的兩隻翅膀旁，想用腳爪幫忙抓著鵬鵬的翅膀好讓他順利飛行。沒想到爸媽的體重太重，鵬鵬又不知道爸媽會這樣突然飛下來幫他，仍然心急的想摸索風的走向，並且用力的鼓動翅膀，一來一往間，「啪！」的一聲後，鵬鵬發出了學飛以來最淒厲的叫聲：「啊……！」

鵬鵬的叫聲驚動了深夜已歸巢的其他大鵬鳥，大家紛紛過來幫忙。鵬鵬的翅膀因為要同時承受父母的體重及拉扯，羽毛四散下，他的翅膀扭傷了！

大家發現鵬鵬的爸媽竟然在深夜裡這樣訓練孩子飛行，紛紛你一言我一語的給起意見來……

「要讓孩子自己練習，不要怕他受傷！以前的父母也沒這樣教我們飛啊，為何要用這樣的方法教孩子？」

「又拉又推，又拴著脖子，這樣要怎麼學飛？這樣哪裡是自己在飛？」

「抓著孩子的翅膀協助孩子飛，這是行不通的，會成為折斷大鵬鳥翅膀的爸媽啊！」

「只要飛得出去，不一定要飛得漂亮！」

「鵬鵬又沒妨礙到別人，就讓他白天練習飛，讓他用自己最舒服的方式去飛。飛是我們大鵬鳥的本能，本能就是要多嘗試、多練習，給那麼多規則怎麼飛？晚上黑漆漆的怎麼飛？」

「陪他啦！看他啦！但不要在旁邊碎念給壓力啦！」

「永遠放不下心，孩子怎麼學飛？現在大鵬鳥越來越少，反而要放手讓孩子磨練，長出自己最好的樣貌，以後一隻大鵬鳥可是要抵十隻大鵬鳥呢！」

鵬鵬的爸媽聽到這些話，忙不迭的將受傷的鵬鵬帶回家！

受傷的鵬鵬從此留在家中休養，內疚的爸媽更勤快的覓食，什麼事也不讓鵬鵬做了！鵬鵬變得只要看見爸媽就將嘴張開，自然會有食物自動掉進嘴裡。

有一天，不知怎的，出外覓食的爸媽一直沒回來，鵬鵬餓得有點受不了，在巢邊探頭探腦的張望，結果發現許多以前的小夥伴正在崖邊飛翔。他們發現鵬鵬，就大聲呼喚他：「快點出來，今天風好大！隨便鼓鼓翅膀就可以飛了！」

「別怕摔，摔了我們幫你頂著啊！」

「你可以自己去找爸媽啊！也可以自己出來找食物！這邊有好多食物喔！」

鵬鵬猶豫了一下，走到崖邊先踩出一隻腳，感受到一股好涼的風！他舒服得瞇起眼睛，不自覺的踏出另一隻腳。一陣大風颳來，鵬鵬的翅膀真的鼓了起來，順著風勢離了崖邊，雖然歪歪斜斜的有點不穩，但，天啊！鵬鵬竟然真的飛起來了！沒有爸媽在旁呵護，鵬鵬真的在飛了！許多友伴圍著他又笑又鳴叫：「對，就是這樣！用心感覺，用心去飛，鵬鵬會飛了！」鵬鵬沒想到飛行原來一點兒也不難！心理障礙一旦突破，就不再是障礙了，這是鵬鵬生為大鵬鳥以來最得意的一天！

鵬鵬的爸媽從此明白要用孩子能接受的方式愛他，才能讓他真正感受到愛。孩子要的可能不是保護，而是讓他們勇敢跨出第一步，要有自己將一件事從頭到尾完成的成就感！最少的協助，或許才能讓大鵬鳥飛出自己最美的姿態。

「教一種學飛的生活態度，而不是一種固定的飛行方式！」

「每隻大鵬鳥只要不妨礙別隻鳥，都可以用自己最舒服的方式過生活！」

「我示範一次，你自己來！讓我看看你自己可以做得多好！」

「陪伴孩子飛，但不要施加壓力跟在旁邊飛。」

「生活就是與自己競爭、和別人合作！」

鵬鵬學飛事件後，這些都成為大鵬鳥鳥族教學的經典名句了。

一定要在最少協助下，自己用心感覺，才能夠學會。可以獨立做一件事的感覺真好！

現在，在許多險峻的崖邊，常可以看到生活得自由自在、神采飛揚，等待起風後可以海闊天空飛行的群鳥之王——大鵬鳥！

• 給教師及家長的話 •

每個人都希望自己的孩子是快樂且成功的，但我們可能要想清楚，是想要孩子一心去追求成功並得到快樂，然而有可能成功後不一定能得到快樂；還是要抱持快樂的心態去做事，進而在成功後同時擁有快樂，熱愛自己所選擇的，然後越快樂越成功。人的一生經歷不同的人事與環境，會有許多外在刺激，然後我們就會有所反應，這是行為學派所常提到的刺激與反應。但人們常常忽略了在刺激與反應間，其實人們是有學習與選擇的成分在中間。如果我們是要讓孩子擁有快樂，能選擇自己所愛而邁向成功，那麼我們可能不只愛孩子，還要懂孩子。愛就是讓孩子自在，愛就是用愛說實話，愛就是給實際的建議，讓孩子自己做決定，在刺激與反應間，做最適性的學習與最自在的選擇。除非是有立即危險性的事情，否則教師與家長應該扮演好支持的角色，鼓勵孩子自我嘗試，多說「Yes」，少說「No」。

我主修的是特殊教育，每天都會見到不少充滿挫折感的孩子，這時教師與家長的教養態度及支持系統就相對重要。在孩子遇到挫折時，我總會鼓勵孩子要想辦法解決問題，因為社會很少會為我們個人而改變。在面對遇到挫折的孩子時，我喜歡跟他們分享這些挫折智商（AQ）：（1）成功者看目標，失敗者看對手；（2）每天都要有微小而明確的進步；（3）如果失敗了就再給自己第二次機會。如同故事中所言，如果學飛是大鵬鳥鵬鵬的目標，那麼如何飛才能自在與成功，或許在外界人事與環境的刺激與反應間，父母更該重視鵬鵬在刺激與反應中間學習與選擇成分發展的可能性。爸媽或許可以協助鵬鵬思考：不一定要很厲害才能開始，可以想成要開始才能變得很厲害；不一定要八成把握才做，或許六成就可以去執行了，然後在做中慢慢調整、學習。

刺激與反應中間的學習與選擇成分也可同時反映在每日的社交技巧上，在處己、處人、處環境的過程中，我覺得較少直接是對與錯的選擇。當然最好的學習與選擇是「你好，我也好」（＋＋）的雙贏狀態；而「我好，你不一定好」（＋－），其實也可以說是合情合理的決定。比較需要

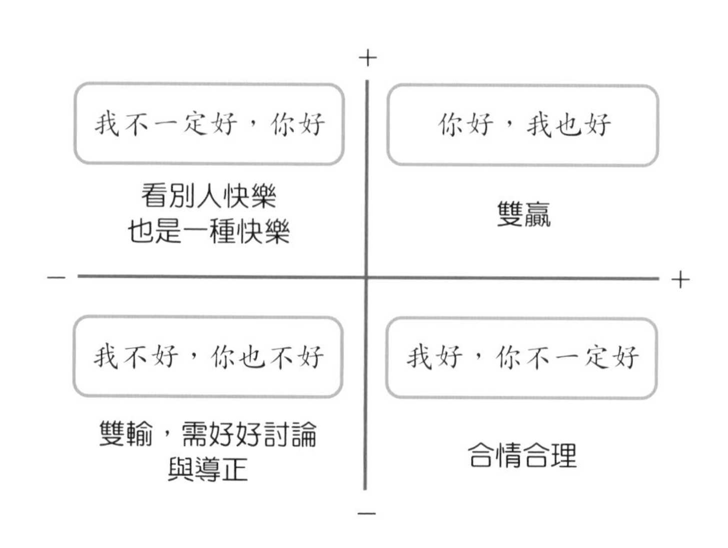

介入處理的或許是「我不一定好，你好」（－＋），則可能需要讓孩子明白看別人快樂也是一種快樂，而這種帶有社會責任的快樂可能是一種無可取代的真快樂。至於「我不好，你也不好」（－－）的雙輸選擇，則需要好好面對孩子討論與導正（參考上頁的象限圖）。

期待這本繪本能讓教師及家長思索在每日生活的刺激與反應中間，學習與選擇成分發展的重要性。我們所要給孩子的是一種自在的生活態度與自主思考能力，而不一定是世俗成功的標準或是絕對對與錯的準則。如前所述，每個人都希望自己的孩子是快樂且成功的人，但是我們要明白，成功後不一定就能得到快樂，應該思考的是如何抱持快樂的心態去做事，進而在成功後同時擁有快樂，熱愛自己所選擇的，才會越快樂、越成功。

Pen Pen Learns to Fly

Written by Ying-Ru Meng
Illustrated by Ning Yan
Translated by Arik Wu

Dapeng bird, a mythical creature in Chinese mythology, is the king of all birds. All the Dapeng birds are gigantic and of green and red feathers.

One well-known Dapeng bird is the one in *Journey to the West*, a Chinese novel written by Wu Cheng-en. The bird in the novel is one of the three demon kings of Lion-Camel State, and is hailed as "the Gigantic Bird of Ten Thousand Cloudy Miles." When he moves, he whips up the wind and stirs up the seas.

Dapeng birds also appear in *Sinbad the Sailor*, but this time they do so under the name Roc. In the story, Sinbad the sailor is abandoned by his shipmen on a remote island during his second voyage. On the island there are quite a number of rocs. Sinbad wittingly ties himself to the leg of a roc and is carried to a mountain valley where there are many rocs' eggs. The eggs are huge, and so are the rocs. They are even big enough to prey on serpents.

During the fifth voyage, Sinbad and his fellow merchants again discover a roc's egg on an island. The merchants disembark the trading vessel to have a closer look at the egg, but end up breaking it and having the baby roc inside as a meal. This breaks parent rocs' hearts. Enraged, they drop enormous rocks from the sky and sink the vessel.

Lastly, Dapeng birds are also praised in one of the poems written by the famous Chinese poet Li Bai, titled "To Li Yong". "The Great Bird one day rises with the wind, and soars ninety thousand miles into the sky," the poem reads. Moreover, there is a Chinese idiom extolling the greatness of Dapeng birds. "Peng-cheng-wan-li", which literally means "the long and ambitious journey of Dapeng birds", is an idiom Chinese people use to wish someone the best of luck in the future.

Dapeng birds used to be such great and incredible creatures, but, as time passes, their habitats have greatly decreased and their population dropped. Also, Dapeng birds need the help of strong wind to take off as they have too big a pair of wings. As a result, they can only live on mountain peaks where the wind is extremely strong and where there is enough space for them to take off.

Such places, however, are harder to come by nowadays. When there is no place for parent Dapeng birds to nest, there is simply going to be less and less baby Dapeng birds. Thus, every baby Dapeng bird that is lucky enough to survive all the hardships naturally becomes the apple of their parents' eyes. Parent Dapeng birds do not even want their precious sons or daughters to take on even the easiest labor. Most baby Dapeng birds, as a result, know nothing about building a nest on their own, and sometimes even fall off the nests during their sleep, hitting the ground and injuring themselves. Worse still, many baby Dapeng birds know not how to hunt serpents, either. They are so horrible at hunting that serpents feel completely safe with their presence, because the serpents know perfectly well that these spoiled baby Dapeng birds are never going to catch them. Having said these, it is still of great importance for baby Dapeng birds to learn how to fly.

Pen Pen, a baby Dapeng bird, is the only child to his parents. Both of them are from prestigious Dapeng families and have been showering Pen Pen with nothing but love and care ever since his birth. Pen Pen, however, is terrible at flying.

Pen Pen's parents, of course, want to help him learn how to fly, but their hands are tied as they are afraid of hurting or injuring him. The more afraid they are, the less likely they are willing to let Pen Pen just go out and practice flying. Gradually, Pen Pen starts losing confidence in himself as a capable Dapeng bird.

Apparently, it takes much longer for Pen Pen to master the art of flying, which, as sad as it may sound, has been quite a disgrace to his parents.

"You see, we little birds fly when we feel like flying and we land when we feel like landing. You Dapeng birds are just so out of luck. You can't take off unless strong wind blows your way and you have to fly at such a high altitude. Birds as small as we are can go everywhere as we please. Up on trees when we are happy, and down on the ground when we feel like it," the small birds living on the mountain peaks cannot help making fun of Pen Pen.

Pen Pen grows more frightened of flying as such ridicule going rampant. Still, he wants to prove himself to be a big bird capable of living on his own. He fans trees with his gigantic wings, and walks around on rocks with his strong legs, trying to tell the world that there is nothing wrong with his body at all. Such actions, however, concern Pen Pen's parents even more.

"Son, listen carefully. We're the king of all birds. Birds can't fly as high as we do, so they don't see the things we see. They are more near-sighted, like some kind of insect that is born in the morning and dies at night and that never gets to experience the change of seasons. We, on the other hand, fly high and see far and wide. We see a world that is completely different, and that means we aren't always understood, but that's fine. Anyway, we'll have more practices tomorrow," Pen Pen's dad says to him in a very serious tone of voice.

Pen Pen's parents worry that their son may be laughed at by other birds, so they wait until night time when all birds go to sleep and start giving Pen Pen lessons about how to fly.

If some bird wakes up and comes out of his nest at night, he will definitely see, in the bright moonlight, one sleepy-looking baby Dapeng bird practicing how to fly with two other grumpy parent Dapeng birds on the mountain peak.

In the past, what parent Dapeng birds did to teach their children how to fly was, for starters, explaining the drills and then pushing them off the cliff right away to let them figure it out themselves. Hitting the ground hard or trapped in the trees growing out of mountainsides was rather common. These baby Dapeng birds never gave up, though. They wiped off the dust and got back on their feet in no time. That was how the generation of Pen Pen's parents learned to fly, through trial and error. Pen Pen's grandparents always told his mom and dad, "Who doesn't fail a couple of times before actually learning how to fly? It's fine as long as you can get back on your feet and give it another try. We're the king of all birds, after all."

However, Pen Pen's parents dare not follow suit, for fear that Pen Pen might accidentally injury himself.

They, therefore, put a rope around Pen Pen's neck in case he falls onto the ground when trying to take off. Pen Pen's dad then holds one end of the rope in his mouth while running toward the cliff for take-off. His mom, on the other hand, pushes him from behind to help him gain the needed momentum. Nevertheless, if Pen Pen does not run fast enough, his neck will be jerked to a suffocatingly uncomfortable angle as his dad is already high up in the air. Also, if his mom pushes too hard from behind, Pen Pen may just trip and hit the ground, getting scratches here and there.

The whole process of learning and teaching how to fly is overwhelmingly tiring. Exhausted, Pen Pen and his parents are often too tired to say anything after countless rounds of practices, and even if there is still some gas left in their tanks, all they do is grumbling or arguing with one another.

This is not going to work, Pen Pen's parents think to themselves. So they decide to give the old way a try. On a moonless night when the wind blows extremely strong, Pen Pen's dad, after giving his son countless instructions, carefully pushes Pen Pen off the cliff, hoping that he will figure it out himself. As soon as Pen Pen falls from the cliff, however, he immediately notices that he has not aligned himself with the direction of the wind. He therefore bursts into screams of fear, crying, "NOOO!"

Upon hearing their beloved son cry out for help, Pen Pen's parents completely forget about the original purpose of this drill and swiftly fly to his sides, hoping to seize him by the wings. Pen Pen, not expecting his parents to come down to help him, is still fluttering his wings by the time they grab him by the wings. The weight of his parents' plus all the jerking and pulling is apparently too much for Pen Pen, which immediately leads to a loud cracking-snapping sound.

"Ouch! It hurts so much!" Pen Pen cries out at the top of his lungs.

The crying of Pen Pen wakes the entire neighborhood up. Every Dapeng bird in the area hurries out of their nests to see what is happening outside. It turns out that Pen Pen, having to bear the weight of his parents and to endure all the pulling and jerking, has strained both his wings.

When everybody discovers that Pen Pen's parents have been secretly giving him lessons about how to fly every night, all of them feel like they need to weigh in on this matter.

"You need to allow him to practice on his own! I'm sure this is not the way our parents taught us how to fly. Why are you doing this to Pen Pen?" one of the Dapeng birds says.

"You can't expect Pen Pen to master the art of flying when there's a rope around his neck and both of you are always there to help him. He has to do it on his own!" another Dapeng bird cuts in.

"It's not going work, you know, seizing him by wings and trying to help him every single time. See? You ended up breaking his wings!" yet another Dapeng bird says.

"I think if he's able to fly, that's good enough already. He doesn't have to fly so gracefully," a Dapeng bird agrees.

"Pen Pen doesn't bother anybody! Just let him practice how to fly during the day and allow him to do it the way he feels most comfortable. Our ability to fly is innate. It's part of our instinct. You've got to allow him the space for trial and error. He isn't going to learn how to fly under so many restrictions, and neither is he going to learn that at night. It's all dark and no light."

"Stay with him and quit all the grumbling and mumbling. It's not helping."

"If you're never going to let go, how is he ever going to learn how to fly? You know, there're fewer of us right now. It's crucial that we allow our children to live the lives they want and be the Dapeng birds they want to be. After all, in the future, one baby Dapeng bird may need to do the work of ten Dapeng birds."

Pen Pen, having strained his wings, is now confined to bed. Feeling quite guilty about the injury, his parents work harder than ever to ensure Pen Pen is well-fed and do everything they can to prevent him from doing any nest chore. Over time, Pen Pen becomes more and more spoiled. Now whenever he feels hungry, he just opens his mouth and expects his parents to feed him.

One day, Pen Pen feels starving, but his parents have not yet returned from hunting. He waits, and waits, and eventually reaches a point where he just cannot wait any longer. He then reaches his head out of the nest, looking around, trying to see if there is any trace of his parents. To his surprise, a lot of his old friends are soaring in the sky. They see Pen Pen from above and immediately call out his name. "Come on out, Pen Pen! The wind today is strong! It'll be a piece of cake for you to take off!"

"Don't be afraid of falling. We'll catch you!"

"Come on out! You can look for your parents yourself, or you can find something to eat out here. There's so much to eat!"

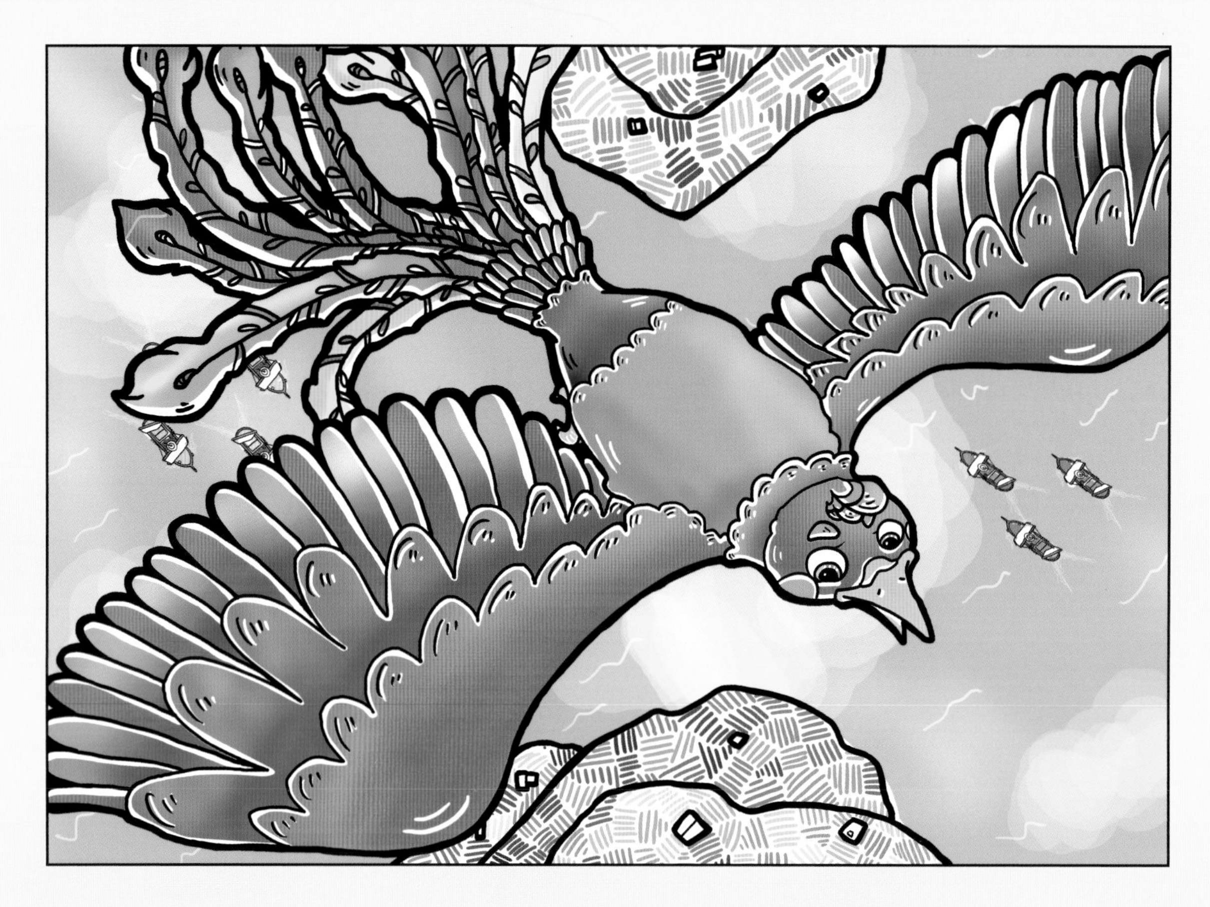

First he is hesitant, but then he manages to step one foot out of the nest. "Oh my, the wind is so cozy and cool," he says to himself. He feels so good that he squints his eyes a little and moves another foot out of the nest. As another wave of wind blows by, Pen Pen feels that his wings are being pushed up. All of a sudden, he actually flies as he goes with the wind. Though looking quite awkward, he is, for the first time of his life, flying without the help of his parents—he is flying on his own!

Many of his old friends honk and cheer around him, looking genuinely excited. "This is it! Feel the wind! You're flying, Pen Pen!" they say.

Pen Pen definitely did not expect things to go so smoothly in the first place. Once he overcomes his mental barriers, he feels like nothing is going to stop him. This has truly been the best and most memorable day in Pen Pen's life!

From then on, Pen Pen's parents understand that it is important to love their child the way he wants to be loved. Pen Pen does not need excessive protection, but the sense of achievement that he is able to get things done from start to finish. Perhaps, only when someone is all on his own, with nearly no help from the outside world, will he become the best version of himself.